TILLY
WITCH

VIKING KESTREL
Viking Penguin Inc., 40 West 23rd Street, New York, New York 10010, U.S.A.
Penguin Books Ltd, 27 Wrights Lane, London W8 5TZ (Publishing & Editorial) and
Harmondsworth, Middlesex, England (Distribution & Warehouse)
Penguin Books Australia Ltd, Ringwood, Victoria, Australia
Penguin Books Canada Limited, 2801 John Street, Markham, Ontario, Canada L3R 1B4
Penguin Books (N.Z.) Ltd, 182-190 Wairau Road, Auckland 10, New Zealand

Copyright © Don Freeman, 1969
All rights reserved
First published in 1969 by The Viking Press
Published simultaneously in Canada
Printed in the United States of America by Horowitz/Rae, Cedar Grove, New Jersey
Library of Congress catalog card number: 72-85867
ISBN 0-670-71303-1
7   8   9   10   11   91   90   89   88   87

TILLY WITCH

BY
DON FREEMAN

The Viking Press   New York

To Susie
and
to Billy

One bright moonlit night, Tilly Ipswitch, Queen of Halloween, stood atop her high mountain peak and sighed, "My, my! What a lovely evening! It makes me feel like being kind to everyone in the world, especially children."

For a wicked witch to have such kindly feelings was, to say the least, quite a switch!

Here it was, nearly Halloween, and Tilly was acting as if she were Queen of the May. Her pet cat, Kit, hid behind a rock and yowled, "Mee-ow! Mee-ouch!"

"Now, Kit," said Tilly, "if boys and girls can have fun pretending to be witches, I don't see why I can't play at being happy and gay, just for a change!"

But later, when Tilly tried to switch back to being a wicked witch again, she couldn't!

She ran inside her house and looked in the mirror. "That's queer!" she said, giggling, "I don't look a bit like my mean old self. Now, how can I frighten children when I feel so good?"

Something certainly had to be done about this, and in a hurry!

Tilly spread out a map on the floor. "Maybe I ought to go see a witch doctor," she told Kit. "I've heard of a Doctor Weegee who lives on this tiny island called Wahoo. They say he cures witches without taking stitches."

Tilly put on a purple dress and dashed down to her broom-port where she kept her new flyer: a surfboard with a whisk broom for a skeg.

"Take good care of the bats and owls, Kit!" she shouted as she sailed into the sky. "I'll be back when I feel worse!"

With the skill of a seasoned surf rider, Tilly rode the crest of the billowy clouds, singing as she streaked along. At last she sighted the small island of Wahoo far below.

After making a happy landing, Tilly danced along to the door
of the witch doctor's hut. But instead of being pleased to see

Tilly in such a giddy mood, Doctor Weegee was horrified.

"Ah Wahee! Ah Hogwash!" he bellowed, which in Wahooese means, "You happy witch! You are very bad!"

Once inside his hut the doctor examined Tilly from the tip of her hat to the tips of her slippers. Finally, he handed her a card on which was written this prescription: MISS FITCH'S FINISHING SCHOOL FOR WITCHES.

Tilly hardly needed to be told what this meant. She had to go back to school, the same school she had attended many years before!

Hopping aboard her surfbroom, she waved a cheery "good-by" and away she flew.

You can imagine Miss Fitch's surprise when she opened the
gate and beheld Tilly Ipswitch, her former prize pupil, stand-
ing there, *smiling*.

Without saying so much as, "How voodoo you do," Miss Fitch led Tilly straight to a classroom where students were busily carving out fierce-looking faces in pumpkins.

Tilly tried her best to be serious but even during the class in Black Magic she simply could not keep from giggling.

Naturally, Miss Fitch was furious, but no matter how much she scolded, Tilly still felt frivolous.

At cooking class that evening, Tilly behaved worse than ever. The student witches were learning how to mix a witch's brew, and each one was taking a turn at adding nasty-tasting things to the pot.

When it came Tilly's turn to show what she could do, she began pouring in syrup and sugar and instant chocolate pudding.

Miss Fitch shrieked. "Go to the corner this minute! And sit facing the wall!"

Poor Tilly was really in disgrace. And as if this weren't punishment enough, she had to wear a tall dunce hat!

For almost an hour, Tilly sat and glowered at the blackboard. Then she began to think about scaring boys and girls. But who would be frightened by a happy witch? They would only *laugh*

at her, or even worse, they might stop believing in Halloween!
The more Tilly thought of this the madder she got and the
madder she got the meaner she felt until

suddenly she spun around, leaped off her stool and started stomping on the dunce hat. "I'm not a dunce!" she screamed, "I'm Queen of Halloween, and I have important duties to attend to!"

Racing outside, she hopped aboard her surfbroom. Miss
Fitch leaned out the window as Tilly sailed away. "Congratula-
tions, Tilly!" she called. "I knew you'd remember your duty.
You're the best student I've ever had!"

Heading straight for home, Tilly stopped only long enough
to pick up a ripe pumpkin from her own pumpkin patch.

As soon as she landed on her mountain peak, she quickly

carved out a ferocious-looking face in the pumpkin. Then, placing it over her head, she crept silently up to her house and slowly opened the creaky door. . . .

"Trick or treat!" she screamed at the top of her lusty lungs.
Poor Kit nearly hit the ceiling!

"Come down, my pet," Tilly coaxed. "See, it's really me, Tilly. I'm ready for Halloween. Come down—we have work to do tonight!"

And so, just about midnight, Tilly and Kit swept across the moonlit sky, riding astride their trusty old broomstick, scaring children everywhere. For Tilly had indeed learned her lesson. As long as Halloween comes once a year you can count on her to be the meanest and wickedest witch in all Witchdom.